DIARY OF A Cricket God

Shamini Flint

Illustrated by Sally Heinrich

ALLEN&UNWIN

SYDNEY • MELBOURNE • AUCKLAND • LONDON

This edition published in 2018

First published in Singapore in 2011 by Sunbear Publishing

Allen & Unwin
83 Alexander Street
Crows Nest NSW 2065
Australia
Phone: (612) 8425 0100
Fax: (612) 9906 2218
Email: info@allenandunwin.com
Web: www.allenandunwin.com

A Cataloguing-in-Publication entry is available
from the National Library of Australia
www.trove.nla.gov.au

ISBN 978 1 74237 826 8

Text design by Sally Heinrich
Cover design by Jaime Harrison
Set in 10/14 pt Comic Sans
This book was printed in June 2020 at SOS Print + Media Group,
63-65 Burrows Road, Alexandria, NSW 2015, Australia.

30 29 28 27 26

For all the kids like Marcus out there

MY CRICKET DIARY

Today is the worst day of
my life EVER.

EVER, EVER, EVER ...

I'm not kidding!!

It's a worse day
than when JT
(the school bully)
hid my clothes
after swimming

... and I had to go to class in my Speedos.

It's a worse day
than when JT
stuck a note on
my back saying
'KICK ME'

... and kids followed me around all day aiming
swipes at my bottom.

It's a worse day than when I scored that own goal with my bottom ... and some smart alec took a photo for the school magazine.

(My *Diary of a Soccer Star* has details of that awful day.)

TODAY IS WORSE THAN ALL THOSE DAYS PUT TOGETHER!!!

You see, Dad's decided that just because I scored in that soccer tournament a few months back (with my feet, not my bottom) that I have a GIFT for SPORT.

Son, you have a gift for sport!

Right, Dad — it was a fluke!!!

He thinks that I have a FUTURE in SPORT.

Get real, Dad — I scored when no one was paying attention — it doesn't mean anything!!!

He thinks Nike or Adidas or Puma might be interested in me ...

PUMA?

Isn't that some sort of mountain lion?
A mountain lion might be interested in me?
Is he threatening me?

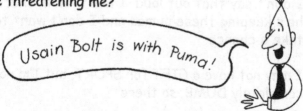

Yes, but Usain Bolt can run really fast! He doesn't have to be afraid.

Is Dad going to feed me to the lions if I don't have a FUTURE in SPORT?

What sort of dad are you???

I don't say that out loud. I don't know where he's keeping these pumas and I don't want to take a chance.

I may not have a GIFT for SPORT, but I'm not completely DUMB, so there.

Back to the reason that this is the WORST DAY OF MY LIFE, EVER …

Dad wants me to play cricket.

Dad wants me to play cricket!!!

What?

Isn't a cricket some sort of insect?

Dad wants me to play a game that's named after an insect?

Everyone loves cricket!

Why, Dad?

One billion people from India love cricket!!

What?

Dad is a marketing guru.

I know that because
it says so on his name
card ...

and on his door,
letterhead,
envelopes and
even a T-shirt
(he had it specially made).

I thought 'marketing' was something you did at the supermarket with Mum.

I thought a 'guru' was some sort of deer.

A marketing guru?
A MARKETING GURU?

What sort of job is that?

Later, Gemma (my older sister) told me that a 'guru' is a teacher.

A 'kudu' is a sort of deer. Easy mistake. Anyone could have made it.

And 'marketing' means being good at selling stuff.

I get it now — Dad teaches people how to sell stuff.

Actually, I don't get it — why does that mean I have to play CRICKET??

Yeah, right.

Dad's written a book called *Pull Yourself Up by Your Own Bootstraps!*

He's always quoting bits from it. It's incredibly ANNOYING.

Actually, I tried the 'you are what you believe' thing.

I believed I was Michael Jackson.

Nope, didn't work.

I believed that JT and I were best mates!!

Nope, that didn't work.

I believed I could fly!!!

Nope, that *really* didn't work.

Dad's at it again...

I wish some of that 'talent' was in my hands and feet.

Even I knew that!!

People buy Dad's book???

Even Spot feels sorry for me.

Spot is my dog.
I love Spot.

Dad got him for me as a reward for doing well in that soccer match where I finally scored a goal (with my foot).

Dad must be pretty desperate — he's offered me a cat, a gerbil, a hamster or a parrot if I agree to try cricket.

Mum looks worried. She thinks our house might turn into a zoo soon.

I don't need any of these other pets.

I have Spot.

But I don't want to disappoint Dad. Not when he's so excited about his son – the FUTURE of SPORT (NOT).

So I agree to give cricket a try.

WILL I EVER LEARN???

Time to begin a new diary.

Even though I hid the last Diary (of a Soccer Star) really well

in a box,

in a bag,

under my bed,

behind a box of old toys,

Gemma still found it.

This time I leave the diary on my desk – but I write MATHS HOMEWORK on the front.

Hidden in plain view.

She'll never find it now.

BWA HA HA HA!!!

And it means I can write that:

My Sister Gemma is ~~A MAJOR NERD~~ A COOL KID

SMELLS like a flower ✿

~~THE WORLD'S BIGGEST PAIN!~~
THE BEST SISTER IN THE WORLD!

She found it and changd all the bits she didn't laik... And fixd the speling!
AAARRGGGHHHH!!!

Dad gets me the cricket kit. It's all white.

Why would anyone play a game in white kit?

Haven't they heard of MUD?

Mum looks depressed. I don't blame her.

She's definitely heard of MUD.

What is all this stuff?

I've never seen anything like it!

It's not kit – it's armour!!

Helmet, elbow guards, back guards, shin guards …

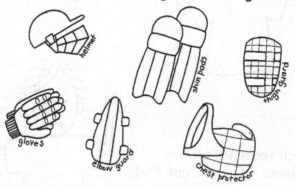

What sort of game is this ANYWAY?

I don't even know where some of these guard things go …

Oh, I see – well, that's just embarrassing!

Dad tried to explain the rules of the game to me:

There are two teams —
Okay, I got that.

Each team has eleven
players — Okay, I got that.

One team bats
and another
team bowls.
BATS? BOWLS?

I was on shaky
ground.

You bat until you're out. Then the other team is in. When they're out, you're back in until you're out again. You have to get the other team out twice while staying in.

Ehhh?

Dad suggested we practise in the garden.

He passed me the ball.

BALL? BALL?? BALL???

It's more like a ROUND BRICK!!

This is a game where people throw
ROUND BRICKS at you.
No wonder everyone
has to wear body armour.

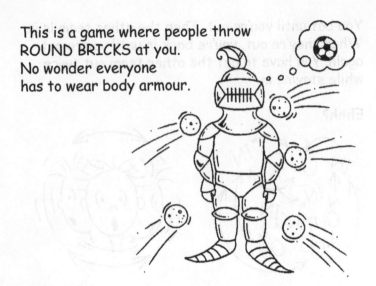

I never thought I'd say this but I actually
miss soccer.

My best friend James came to visit.

Are you a bowler?

I thought a bowler was a type of hat like
Thomson and Thompson wear in *Tintin?*

Apparently the stick thing is called a bat. Duh!

Dad throws the ROUND BRICK – the ball – at me, bowls it at me, I mean.

Well, now I understand all the equipment anyway – even that last bit.

I swung the bat as hard as I could.

 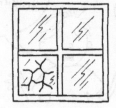 

One window, two windows, three windows later ...
Mum came out of the house.

For once, it was Dad in trouble, not me.

And then I heard the words I've been dreading ...

The last time I had a coach, for soccer, it was a nightmare.

Nope, I don't think coaching is a good idea at all.

BUT WHO CARES WHAT I THINK???

My first lesson was bowling...

My new team-mates seemed to find this very funny.

I wasn't sure why.

Later, Dad told me that Muttiah 'Murali'
Muralitharan and Shane Warne were the greatest
spin bowlers ever.
Spin bowlers?

How do you spin and bowl at the same time?

I'd be lucky not to hurt someone!!

Coach asked me if I wanted to bat or bowl ...

I remembered
the windows,
so I said bowl.

Spin or fast?

Eh?

Are You a
SPIN bowler
or a
FAST bowler?

Well, for sure, I knew I wasn't a spin bowler.
(See above.)

The coach was turning red, so I picked up the ball and threw it at the batsman.

I knew it would be hard, but I never guessed it would be as hard as this …

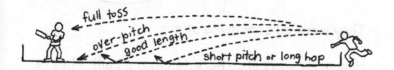

Last lesson, I noticed a really strange thing ...

The team worked really hard to keep the ball clean. They kept wiping it on their trousers. It was weird. I know Mum would prefer that the trousers stayed clean and the ball stayed dirty ...

I grabbed the ball and wiped it on my trousers. I didn't want to get into any more trouble!

They were all screaming at me.

How many ways are there to clean a ball? They're fussier than Mum!

Later Dad told me that you're only supposed
to rub one side of the ball so it gets shiny.
This helps the ball swing.

Well, I should have guessed
that – NOT!

Do I look like some sort
of scientist???

Coach told me to bat.

So I stood there holding the bat while balls whizzed all around me.

It was the SCARIEST experience of my life!

Finally, I swung
the bat and it caught
the ball, which flew straight
into a fielder's hands.

Coach put his finger in the air.

I wondered what he was pointing at.

I looked up.
Maybe there was
a bird or a plane
or something ...

When I looked back, Coach had turned red.
(All my coaches seem to do that.)

No, I haven't – no one's caught me and I'm not
even running.
Is JT around???

Spencer 'Boom Boom' Harris explained that if you hit the ball and someone catches it before it hits the ground, the batsman is out. Pointing a finger in the air is the way umpires signal to a batsman that he's out.

'Out' is definitely safer than 'In'.

Coach made me bat again.

Spencer was bowling. This time the ball went under my bat, through my legs and hit those sticks with the bits of wood on top.

Again ...

Great Yorker, Spencer!

Is Spencer from New York?

YOU'RE OUT!!!

HURRAY!

'Out' is definitely safer than 'In'!

Later Dad tells me that those stick things at the end are called stumps. If the ball, bat or any part of your body hits the stumps, the batsman is OUT.

He also tells me that a 'yorker' is a full-length delivery. Duh.

I'm STUMPED why anyone would want to play this dumb game!

Back to training ...

I made some real progress!

I finally hit the ball
with the bat!!

Is JT around?

Later Dad tells me that, in cricket, you and the other batsman have to run between the wickets.

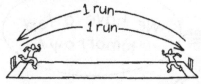

And each run is like a point.

Unless you hit the ball to the boundary ...

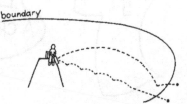

Then it's four runs.

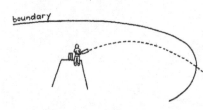

Unless the ball flies over the boundary without touching the ground ...

Then it's a six (six runs).

Who makes this stuff up? Runs, fours, sixes?

Luckily, I'm good at maths so I can add all these runs up.

Not that I have to do that, as I don't actually hit the ball again that day.

Dad just told me that a test is what you call a match or a game in cricket.

HOW WAS I SUPPOSED TO KNOW THAT??

So there's a friendly cricket game — sorry, I mean TEST — tomorrow. Our team against some kids from the school across the road.

I just can't believe it. It's happening again!!!

Don't they know that I'm Marcus 'Talk to the Bottom' Atkinson???

Dad's not happy that I'm not in the team.

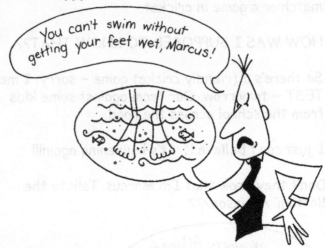

You can't swim without getting your feet wet, Marcus!

Right, Dad. I don't mind putting my feet in the water. It's having my bottom in the school newspaper I don't like.

WEEKLY NEWS
MARCUS SCORES!
GOAL OF THE MATCH

REMEMBER??

Anyway, I'm not in the team so it can't happen again. Right? Right?? RIGHT???

I've just been told that LBW means 'leg before wicket'.

You're not allowed to protect the wicket with your legs – only the bat.

If the ball hits you on the legs in front of the wicket – you're out.

Fair enough – anyway, not my problem, since I won't be in the team!!! RIGHT???

Unfortunately, Boom Boom (Spencer) came down with a cold the evening before the game.

DO I LOOK
LIKE I CARE???

Game time ...

We were down to ten men. All our other players
were out except Tom 'KP' Plate.

Coach sent me on.

That didn't seem too hard.
I just had to stand there, stop the ball from
hitting the stumps and not get caught.
RIGHT.

I saw Jack 'the Brute' Montgomery come racing up ...

He had the ball — that ROUND BRICK — in his hand.

The Brute is the fastest bowler in his school.

He bowled the ball at me ...

I panicked. (You would have too!)

I dropped the bat. (You would have too!!)

I turned around. (You would have too!!!)

THE BALL HIT
MY BOTTOM!!!

(Why does that ALWAYS happen to me?)

A camera flashed.

The finger went up. (This time
I didn't look up to see what the
umpire was pointing at.)

You guessed it — back on the front page of the school newspaper.

I was out, not LBW but BBW!!

Time to spend an awful lot of time in my room with a paper bag over my head ...

Hasn't this happened before?

The next weekend, I didn't want to go for training.

Who would?

Not Marcus 'BBW' Atkinson, that's for sure.

Son, when you fall off a bike, you've got to get back on again!

Right, Dad. And when I fall off my bike, I'll be sure to do that. But this is CRICKET!!!

I don't say that out loud. I don't want to upset Dad any further.

It can't be easy being my dad.

Not if you want to sell T-shirts.

Maybe if you wanted to sell bloopers videos.

Finally, Dad said I could take Spot with me to cricket to keep me company.

I'm put in to bat again.

Shaun 'Fingers' Wayne is bowling.

First ball:

Great googly, Fingers!

Eh?

The ball spins past me.

Second ball:

The ball spins past me the other way.

Great Chinaman, Fingers!

Eh?

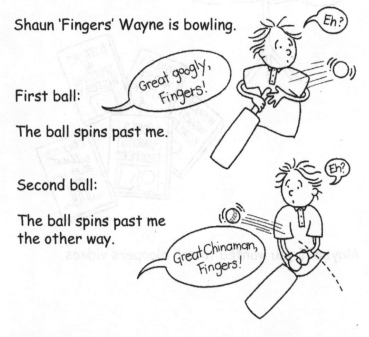

(Mum would never let me say anything like that.)

Third ball:

I'm through the shot long before
the ball arrives.

(Are they talking about dolphins?)

Fourth ball:

The ball spins right past the bat.

(Who are they calling a wrong 'un?)

Fifth ball:

I remembered to set out for a RUN.

I was going to score a RUN!

MY first RUN ever!!

Spot, who was looking very bored, suddenly raced after the ball.

Spot grabbed the ball and ran back to the crease.

I was halfway across.

Spot dropped the ball.

A fielder picked it up and knocked off the bails.
That means I'm out too.

Great fielding, Spot!

Yeah thanks, Spot!

Yes, thanks, Spot. How come you're playing for the
other team? You're supposed to be MY dog.

Who's he calling a DUCK?

A DUCK!!!

Eh?

Later Dad explained that a 'duck' was when a batsman was out without scoring a run.

In that case, I'm a whole flock of ducks. I just wish I could fly away for the winter and escape from the game of cricket!!!

And the rest? Dad explained that 'googlies' and 'flippers' and 'wrong 'uns' and 'Chinamen' were just different ways of bowling the ball. DUH.

Where do they get these names anyway?

Dad wasn't sure, except that he thought a 'googly' was named after the goggle-eyed expression on a batsman's face when he didn't know which way the ball was going.

That would have been me, then.
Mind you, if it was based on my expression, every single ball bowled in cricket EVER would be called a GOOGLY. So there.

Things got worse ...

Did the coach just call me silly? Just because I can't play his DUMB game??

Boom Boom whispered that it meant I had to field at silly point.

Like that helped.

He dragged me by the arm and showed me where I was supposed to crouch and catch the ball.

It didn't take me long to figure out why the position was known as SILLY point.

I really can't believe Dad's making me play cricket.

I haven't scored a goal — a run, I mean — yet.

I'm back in the school papers. Well, my bottom is anyway.

Spot is more popular than I am.

And he's a better fielder.

And my head is sore where I got hit by the ball.

SILLY is just about right ...

Dad, the marketing guru, said:

> CHAPTER 4
> There's no point crying over spilt milk

He's right, of course. There's no point crying over spilt milk. Well, unless you're my little sister, Harriet, and it's your dinner ... or you're a cat.

But I'm not upset about spilt milk, am I?

I'm upset about making a complete and utter IDIOT of myself!!!

I took Spot for training the next day as well. At least he's company for when I get out.

This time Coach made me bowl again. You're supposed to bowl six times in a row unless you bowl a no ball.

First ball: My arm was crooked. No ball.

Second ball: I stepped over the line. No ball.

Third ball: I bowled a beamer (threw it straight at the other guy). No ball.

Fourth ball: I bowled a wide
(too far from the player to hit).
No ball.

Fifth ball: Too high. No ball.

Sixth ball: I bowled a proper delivery! The
batsman hit it.

A couple of fielders ran after it.

It was in the air.

Maybe they'd catch it and
I'd get my first wicket!!!

I'd forgotten about Spot.

This is not a game
of fetch, Spot!

He looked at me.

Spot charged away after the ball. I watched him
with horror.

I thought he'd understood.

Spot leapt in the air and caught the ball in his mouth.

He looked at the two fielders running towards him.

SIX!!!

He ran right over the boundary rope and dropped the ball on the ground.

SIX!!!

Why does Spot always play for the other team?

Desperate times call for desperate measures ...

All right, Mum wants to play tough ...

Fine, I know what will work.

This is a huge offer, because
Gemma makes a real mess of it —
she never knows where the pieces go and she can't
follow the instructions.

Mum tried.

Maybe not — but I'm pretty sure Rome was built quicker than the time it's going to take me to learn how to play cricket. So there!!!

Next coaching session ...

I hit the ball.

We all looked around to see where it had gone.

There was no sign of it.

Very funny (NOT!). Aren't they tired
of this joke yet?

I hit the ball again.

This time I knew what to expect.

I looked up. Sure enough, the ball was hurtling down at me.

I caught it.

OUT!

I was just protecting my head!!!

Later, Dad told me that if a batsman catches the ball, he's out. Even if he's just protecting his head from serious injury.

Go figure. Is this cricket or the army?

Lizzie (from soccer) came to visit.

In her Liverpool shirt.

Doesn't she have any other clothes??

Lizzie eats, sleeps and breathes soccer.

We have another match. This time Coach doesn't pick me.

Thank goodness.

But Dad is like a bear with a sore head. (Or me trying to play cricket.)

He's like someone with ants in their pants. (Or me trying to bowl.)

He needs to hold his horses!!!

BTW, we're learning English idioms at school.

That's the plan, Dad!

(I didn't say that out loud. Dad's upset enough. It would be like a red rag to a bull.)

I would, Dad — if it was an extra mile away from cricket.

I didn't say that out loud either.

And pigs might fly, Dad.

(Coach didn't actually say any of this, but I could read his mind. It's not difficult when you're Marcus 'BBW' Atkinson.)

Only Spot understands how I feel.

The match is in two days.

I'm having kittens.

Dad is very excited.

I must be adopted.

Maybe there was a mix-up at the hospital when I was born?

Probably the real Marcus is out there somewhere being forced to play computer games ...

Sebastian came to visit.

His dad has given up trying to make him play sport.

How did you get him to do that?

He heard the soccer coach...

Are you really that hopeless or did you have lessons?

That wouldn't work with Dad.

CHAPTER 19

There's no such thing as failure.

There was a new kid at cricket today – Hari Sreenivasan.

He was short, wore glasses and had a book under his arm.

I thought he'd be hopeless.

He wasn't.

It was like watching Luke Skywalker bat.
The Force was strong in this one.

Later, I noticed the book was called *1000 Ways to Bat*. Hari knew at least 999 of them.

The other kids called him 'The Littlest Master', whatever that means.

Later Dad told me that the greatest batsman of all time, Sachin Tendulkar, is called 'The Little Master'.

I bet he sells a lot of T-shirts ...

I asked Hari ...

How'd you get to be so good?

My Dad used to bowl at me when I was a small kid ...

I was really tempted to blame my dad because I can't bat (or bowl).

But it wouldn't be fair.

You see — Dad did try.

When I was three, Dad used to roll balls to me ...

Kick it, Marcus!

It was more like bowling than soccer.

When I was four, he tried throwing balls at me ...

Mum stopped him when he knocked me out cold.

When I was five, Dad gave me a hockey stick ...

I broke his toe.

When I was six ... enough already!
You get the picture.

And he still hasn't given up hope.

CHAPTER 11

Where there's life there's hope.

The day before the game, the kittens have had babies.

Coach told us that a big crowd was expected to the game.

Why?

Apparently, they want to see what I do next.

Hey, Marcus! We're going to come along tomorrow!

I'm a celebrity – get me out of here!!!

I'm a real-life bloopers video.

The kittens have brought their friends and relatives ...

Only one thing can save me now. If it rains, the game will be called off.

The rain dance didn't work.

Mum, Dad, Gemma, Harriet, Sebastian, Lizzie, JT, my teacher and even Spot had come to watch.

There wasn't a cloud in the sky. Useless rain dance.

Coach tossed a coin. The Littlest Master called 'heads'.

It was 'tails' and we had to bowl first. I was in the field – as far away from the action as possible.

Heads!

But it was like I was a magnet to the ball.

The batsman hit it ...

The ball slipped through my fingers. Four.

The batsman hit it ...

The ball hit me on the head and bounced over the boundary. Six.

The batsman hit it ...

The ball rolled between my legs. Four.

Drinks break.

You need to stop watching the fantasy cricket in your head, Dad.

Coach put me in to bowl. He must really want that new kit.

One over, six balls, thirty-six runs.

One over, six balls, THIRTY-SIX RUNS!

ONE OVER, SIX BALLS, THIRTY-SIX RUNS!!!

Even JT wasn't laughing.

Dad wasn't smiling. (There's no such thing as failure, Dad???)

Coach was red and mad.

Only Spot licked my hand.

Our team needed one hundred and thirty-six runs to win. In ten overs.

But we had The Littlest Master.
He waved that bat around like a light sabre.
The scoreboard was ticking over nicely.
But at the other end, batsmen were falling like flies ...

Well, it's nice that the team agreed with me for once.

We needed five runs to draw, six runs to win.
There were six balls left.

Unfortunately, I was at the batting end.

Just try and get a single!

I understood what Hari wanted. If I got a single, he would bat, get the six and we would win.

If I got out, we would lose.

If I didn't score any runs, we would lose.

No pressure!!!

First ball: I missed it.

Second ball: I missed it.

Third ball: I missed it.

Fourth ball: I missed it.

Fifth ball: I missed it.

Just one more ball.

I had to score a six now to win
the game.

NO CHANCE.

The Littlest Master was
leaning on his bat looking
depressed.

After the game, I'm going to go looking for my
real parents.

The bowler came running in.
I swung the bat as if my life depended on it.

(Maybe it did, you should have seen Coach's face when I missed the first five balls.)

I heard the beautiful sound of leather on willow.

Everyone looked in the air.

Was it a four?

WAS IT A SIX?

I looked down. Hari was right. I must have caught an inside edge and the ball had flown into my POCKET.

I reached down ...

That's right – if I handled the ball, I was out.

The other team had figured out where the ball was.

They were starting to walk towards me.

Once they got their hands on the ball, that was it.
Game over.

I heard Spot. He probably thought I was in danger from all those fielders.

I remembered how Spot had scored a SIX for the other team during training.

He'd carried the ball over the boundary …

He'd carried the BALL over the BOUNDARY!

I ran for the boundary.

The ball was still in my pocket.

The fielders gave chase.

The crowd was screaming.

I jinked from side to side.

Tackles were flying in.

GAP

The other team was blocking my way.

I spotted a gap.

Dived for the line.

The ball trickled out of my pocket.

Coach was smiling. Dad was smiling. JT was smiling.

We won the game by one run.

Thanks to Spot.

Maybe I'm not adopted, after all.

Unfortunately, now that I've scored the winning runs, Dad will probably make me play cricket for the rest of my life ...

Son, I think you're right...

...cricket is not your game.

I don't have to play cricket?

About the Author

Shamini Flint lives in Singapore with her husband and two children. She is an ex-lawyer, ex-lecturer, stay-at-home mum and writer. She loves cricket!

www.shaminiflint.com

Have you read my Soccer Diary?

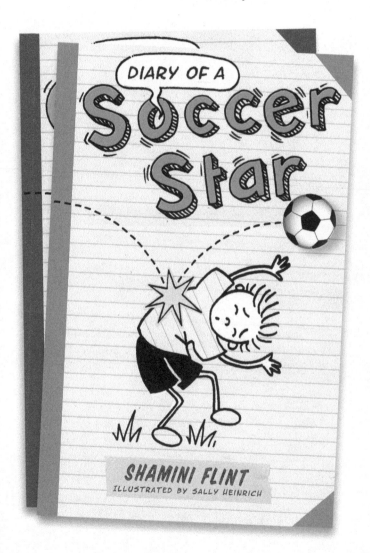